SUNSHINE
AND THE
STALKER

A Live Write by

Dani René *and* K Webster

Sunshine and the Stalker

Dating is difficult for someone like me.
I'm obsessive, arrogant, and rude.
This means I must be creative
when bedding a woman.
I learn what I can about her
through whatever means necessary.
Some call it stalking. I call it clever research.
It gets me what I want and when I want it.
When I get bored, I move on.
My system works like a charm…
Until a little ray of
SUNSHINE
shows up.

Dating is nonexistent for me.
I'm quirky, silly, and inexperienced.
This means my romantic life is certainly lacking.
I don't date because no one's interested.
Some say I'm an independent woman
who doesn't need a man.
But I know I'm on the fast track
to becoming a lonely cat lady.
How many cats are too many cats anyway?
My boring world stays that way…
Until my future stepmother's
STALKER
shows up.

CHAPTER ONE

❧

JAMES

I'M A BIT OF A STALKER, I'LL ADMIT. I HAVEN'T always been this way. At one time, I was a normal forty-something-year-old man who dated the regular way. Awkward Tinder meetups. Lunch dates with stuffy businesswomen. Casual drunk fucks at nightclubs or bars. But no matter how much I "dated," I was unsatisfied. I would grow bored of the woman mid-fuck because I'm a hard man to please.

Which is why I began something new last year . . .

No longer do I fish for women and hope I find a great catch.

Now, I hunt.

Something about the hunt makes the kill so much sweeter. Not an actual kill, of course. A metaphorical kill, if you will. I prowl in the shadows after meticulous searches where I learn about my newest interest. Her schedule. Her favorite restaurant. The way she smiles bright and brilliant for some and forced for others. It's addicting, and now that I've started, I can't stop. I eventually insert myself into their lives, make a move they can't resist, and then they're a good run for a few months.

I've perfected it.

One hundred percent fail proof.

The newest woman is named Olivia. Tall, blonde, bright-blue eyes. That's my type. And, fuck, if she doesn't have the longest legs I've ever seen. I can't wait to lure her into my bed and have those perfect legs wrapped around my waist as I drive into her. I love it when they scream my name.

James. James. You're a sex beast, James.

Tonight is the night where I make my move.

I've learned all there is to know about her.

We're going to fuck. And soon.

Olivia climbs out of an expensive car

and is met by the doorman to her building. He takes her things, and she lifts her chin in a confident way. Everything about her screams sex and power and perfection. Perhaps she could be the one. One day, I'll find the right "one" and settle.

"Hey, dude," a young voice chirps from behind me. "She's kind of a psycho. I've seen you around, hiding in the shadows, which I'll admit is kind of creepy, even for me, watching her. Liv puts on a great face for the world, but behind closed doors, she's a total bitch."

Irritation rises inside me hot and fast. Getting caught isn't something that happens. Ever. And now some teenage boy thinks he can fuck with something I've been working on for months?

Fuck him.

I swivel around, taking my eyes off the perfect Oliva and glower at him.

Except he's not a him.

He's a her.

A very, very, very short her.

My eyes skim over her youthful features. Too young for my tastes, but I take the moment to inspect her with a scrutinizing glare. Her eyes are big and amber, the color of honey. Thick black lashes blink at me, seemingly unafraid of my blatant staring. I skim past her admittedly cute upturned nose sprinkled with freckles.

Her lips though . . .

The moment she smiles, a little crooked, and reveals all her pearly whites, I blink in confusion.

Who is this girl, and why does she have me pinned down in this moment as though she is the hunter and I the prey?

Ridiculous.

"My dad is dating Liv," she explains as snow begins to fall and dusts her purple beanie she wears on top of her head. From beneath the hat, dark red hair slides past her shoulders. Thick streaks of black are mixed in. What strange-colored hair. "I'm just doing you a solid," she says, grinning again. Then, she does a small wave before pushing past me. "Peace out, stalker man."

As though she holds an invisible rope, I find myself following her into the expensive building. Olivia is long gone, and I can't find it in me to worry about that right now. Currently, I need to know who this girl is and why she has such power over me.

This is madness.

She wears an ugly yellow pea coat that hangs well past her waist, hiding her ass from me. Beneath the coat is a black-and-white polka-dot dress. The tights she wears with it are pink, and she finishes off the look with black combat boots.

What kind of weird-ass fucking outfit is she wearing?

And yet I continue to follow her.

She pushes a button on the elevator, and when it opens, we step inside. Her head bobs to a beat that doesn't match the elevator music as she pushes 14 on the panel.

"I told Dad I wanted to live on the fourteenth floor because it's technically the thirteenth floor if you actually count them." She lets out a cute laugh. "And how cool is that? I live on the real thirteenth floor. I'm not superstitious, so it's awesome."

Her babbling should be annoying, but her throaty voice, which I originally assumed belong to a boy, has me hanging on her every word. Sultry and seductive. Rich and decadent. Not high-pitched at all, but a little on the deeper, sexier, real woman kind of way.

"How old are you?" I demand, my voice cold and harsh, just like me. When I'm not participating in my hunting games and playing a part to get what I want, I'm kind of an asshole. So I've been told.

She arches a brow and smirks. "Eighteen going on old cat lady. Black cats are my thing. Told you I wasn't superstitious. What is the magical number before you're officially a cat lady anyway? I have four. Four is still normal, right? Like I'm not going to turn off potential love interests when Beavis, Butt-Head, Snoopy, and Hank come circling his ankles the moment he steps into my apartment, right? Right?"

I stare at her. Her mouth keeps moving, but I don't hear any of the words. Just the sultry, seductive way she says them. My cock has taken an interest in this bizarre woman much sooner than my brain has. My brain thinks she's a ridiculous, talkative, horribly dressed child.

So why am I following her?

The elevator doors open, and she walks through them, not at all frightened that some six-foot-three angry asshole in a power suit is prowling behind her, desperate for some unknown fucking reason to yank her hat off and touch her silky red-and-black hair.

"You're officially the creepiest man I have ever met," she chirps as though she meets creepy people all the time and befriends them. She digs into her deep coat pockets and pulls out an obnoxious mess of key chains. All for two keys. Insanity. Utter insanity.

"James," I grunt. "James Darden."

"As in the Darden Hotel across the street?" She turns and regards me. Her head cocks to the side as she inspects me.

"I know where you live now," I blurt out. This is another reason why I don't date the normal way. Normal isn't even in my vocabulary. Structured and planned and rehearsed is because I say inappropriate shit sometimes.

She laughs and shakes her head. "And the cat lady is officially not the weirdest person on this block anymore. Congratulations, Darden, you're the winner."

Her wink is the last thing I'm gifted of her before she pushes into her apartment and shuts the door behind her.

What the fuck have I just gotten myself into?

CHAPTER TWO

CERYS

THE APARTMENT IS EMPTY WHEN I STEP inside, my body still affected by the stalker who followed me to the door. There was something about him. A hint of need. Hunger that he didn't hide very well. Even though he regarded me with an inkling of desire in his eyes, I wasn't scared. In fact, I wanted to see what he would do.

Most men are controlled, and I thought he was, but as soon as he laid those dark eyes on me, all I could see was how badly he wanted to touch me. Perhaps even lean in and sniff me.

Chuckling, I head into my bedroom and pull off my combat boots. The pink tights I'm wearing find a place on the floor quickly along with my dress. Sitting on my double bed with purple polka-dot bedding, I glance at my pale skin and wonder if I'll ever get a tan. Living in this city, I think not. Winters here are long and icy, which only makes me want to hide away.

I wonder if the stranger would've noticed me if I didn't speak to him first. Would he approach me? I glance at my full-length mirror and shake my head. No. Why would he look at me when Olivia is beautiful and perfect?

My phone rings then, and I find Daddy's name on the screen flashing at me with a warning. I know why he's calling. It's the same thing every time.

"Hey, Dad," I answer with a smile, holding out hope he's going to tell me he's coming home for dinner.

"Hey, pumpkin, listen. I'm stuck at the office tonight. I'm so sorry," he apologizes, the same way he does every night. At least, since Mom died, he's been staying at the office more often than not. When he met Olivia, I thought things would change, but no. There's nothing that would make my father be the man he used to be.

He's long gone, and I know I have to get over it. I have to grow up, but I miss him.

"That's fine, Dad. I'm heading out with Kia, is that okay?" I don't know why I ask him. He doesn't care. He wouldn't even notice if I spent the night out. I go to sleep, and he's not home; I wake up, and he's never here.

"Yes, honey. I'm sorry," he repeats. I know he is. He's always sorry, but that doesn't help. I nod, blinking back the tears threatening to fall. I don't cry. I never even cried when Mom died. I stood by and watched her coffin lower, and I walked away.

Perhaps I'm broken. Maybe there's

something wrong with me.

"It's fine, Daddy. I'll see you tomorrow," I tell him, knowing I won't. I don't see him much, except for weekends when he's not working and has no excuse to be at the office. But even then, he spends his time with Liv.

"I promise, pumpkin. You're not angry, are you?"

"No, Dad. I'm eighteen, old enough to look after myself," I inform him confidently. Because I am. I don't need him watching my every move, but I would like it if he just offered me support, love. Something.

Perhaps I need a man. A sugar daddy to look after me. I giggle at the thought. "Love you, Dad," I say before hanging up. I don't need him to tell me he loves me, but I know he needs to hear it from me. I've known it since I was a kid.

The thought returns. A sugar daddy. But the thing is, I don't need money, I just need love. Someone to show me I matter to them. I crave love, affection, and perhaps my sexual drive is through the roof, but I'd love to have a man show me real pleasure.

I head to the patio and stare out the window, noticing more of the white shit falling.

I hate snow.

I hate winter.

It's shitty.

But since Olivia already lived here, of

course Daddy wanted to be near her. He'd do anything for her. But his own daughter is a pain in his ass. Sighing, I make my way to my bathroom and brush my teeth. I glance in the mirror. The pink hue on my cheeks makes me smile. At least there's some color to my rather pale skin. Once I've freshened up, I head back to my bedroom and flop on the bed. I stare at the ceiling, thinking about the weird stranger who followed me all the way to the thirteenth floor.

Fucking weirdo. Hot. But still a weirdo.

I glance at the time on my alarm clock on my nightstand. It's only ten, and I know Saskia will be here soon. My best friend is a crazy bitch who loves to drag me to clubs with her. She has a thing for college boys, but me, I prefer more distinguished men.

Like James Darden.

Not that I've ever had a man. Or boy for that matter.

Yeah, eighteen-year-old virgin over here. But don't shout it out to everyone. Being a hipster with tomboy tendencies hasn't allowed me the attention of any boys at school. My focus has always been my studies and my art.

Most kids my age have no idea what they want to do. I knew the moment I hit thirteen. The paints and canvases Daddy bought me sit in a studio he specially gifted me when I turned sixteen. It's my space. A place where I can be who I really am.

Someone like James Darden would never be interested in a tomboy hippie with a love for art and crazy artists like Dali and Picasso. No, he's after someone like my soon-to-be step-mother. Even though they haven't sealed the deal, because that's what it would be, I know she'll take Dad for everything he has.

Don't get me wrong. He seems happy, but the bitch is like Cruella de Ville. She's successful in her own right, but there's something cagey about her. She'd be one of those evil stepmoms who want nothing more than your father's affection but feels threatened by you. I've seen enough fucking Disney movies to know they're never good.

I wish things were simpler. I wish my dad didn't need a woman in his life, but then again, I can't wish that on him, because I want someone in my life.

I have my best friend, but she's a girl. I need a man. A real man.

My phone vibrates wildly on the nightstand, snagging my attention. When I pick it up, there's a message from an unknown number. Swiping the screen, I open the message app to find the stalker's initials as a sign off on the two-sentence warning.

When I find something I want, I don't stop until I get it. You, my dear, are something I want. - JD

It should scare me, but fuck, I'm so far

from afraid. In fact, I want him to come here right now and show me exactly what he's capable of.

I tap out a reply and hit send.

Empty threats don't scare me, Stalker.

I drop the phone on the bed beside me and get up. Finding a black, figure-hugging dress, I slide it on and glance in the mirror.

I'm just zipping up the side of my dress when the doorbell dings loudly. I know it's probably my best friend, so I race to get it. I pull open the door, but the face on the other side is not Saskia at all. No. It's someone who shouldn't be here.

James Darden.

CHAPTER THREE

JAMES

MONEY BUYS ANYTHING THESE DAYS. Sold-out tickets to concerts. Homes that aren't for sale. Positions and power and a whole slew of other things. But what it buys me, that I find ridiculously important, is information.

Olivia Castle is a thing of the past. A forgotten craving. An inkling of a desired moment that doesn't matter anymore.

In her place is Cerys Youngblood.

Those amber eyes haunted me from the moment she closed her door until now. Like a maddening disease, everything I'd learned about her in a few short moments festered and grew and spread inside me. The desperation to learn more was real. A voracious need to cut her life open with a scalpel and take my time removing every vital piece of her world, inspecting each part with careful scrutiny.

This obsession is alarming.

I tend to stalk and follow and cross lines, but this is utterly unidentifiable in my mind.

Something that makes zero sense in my head.

All it took was a walk back to the hotel, emptying my safe, and taking every goddamned hundred-dollar bill I had on me at the moment for the doorman to sing like a motherfucking canary. Turns out, he was a wealth of information. Less than an hour, and I had all I needed to know that I was going to make her mine.

But it was her reply to my text only a few moments ago that sent me over the edge.

Empty threats don't scare me, Stalker.

Whatever shred of control I'd been holding onto snapped and sent me damn near charging to her apartment door. I'm practically twitching with need as I wait for her to answer.

So trusting, this little girl with the strange name and strange hair and strange clothes.

So trusting and innocent.

Just waiting to be victimized by my expertise in the bedroom.

I want to possess and consume her unlike any woman I've ever encountered.

And when I finally have her, I will punish her for this power she has over me. I'll extract the cries from her body with physical pain mixed with pleasure as she's been the sadist wreaking havoc in my mind. It's only fair. Tit for tat.

When she opens the door, I'm not fully prepared for what I see. I expected more bizarre clothing. Mismatched colors and fabrics. Styles from one era that don't even belong in the same room as styles from another era.

Yet now?

Now she is timeless in her simple black dress.

Somehow a classic beauty transcending every level of time.

I'm struck senseless.

Anger wells up inside of me. How dare she lure me in like this and take me by surprise? How dare she ruin my careful planning and execution? How dare she tempt me into making a goddamn fool of myself because I don't have a plan?

Her smile catches me off-guard and snuffs out my fury. I find myself stepping closer and closer and closer until I'm peering down at her honey eyes and my fingers are wrapping around her red-and-black locks.

She smells like innocence and flowers.

Like youth and freedom and everything but me.

I want to stain her with reality.

Mark myself on every part of her.

Make her realize the world is much darker than she knows.

"Creeper alert," she murmurs, her voice flirty and carefree.

"I'm in your home, and you are not afraid," I growl, inhaling her.

She presses a palm to the center of my chest over my tie and pushes slightly. Not enough to force me away but enough to keep me momentarily from mauling her.

"Slow down, tiger."

"Trusting strangers is dangerous," I bite out, my tone harsh and condescending.

She smiles, her honey eyes dancing with interest. "But we've already met, Stalker Darden. We're hardly strangers anymore."

Something rubs against my leg, and I jerk back to find a black cat staring up at me. I wonder if this beast knows this is a fifty-four-hundred-dollar custom-made Tom Ford suit. He lets out an unimpressed "meow" and continues his relentless rubbing.

"Hank is a texture man," Cerys explains as if this makes all the sense in the world.

It makes zero sense.

This world of hers she's drawn me into is like some alternate reality.

Like the *Alice and Wonderland* Broadway show I saw once. Talking cats and psychedelic drugs. An upside-down world of sorts.

"Why are you dressed like this?" I demand, ignoring her strange words.

She laughs and shakes her head. "I was going out. To the club with my friend, if you must know, *Dad*."

I sneer at her mocking words, but my cock lurches in my slacks. "You're not going anywhere, Alice."

Her eyebrow arches. "The name is Cerys."

"I know, *Alice*. Now call your friend and

tell her plans have changed."

A rosy pink color blooms across her slender throat when I close the door behind me. I turn the lock, nudge the cat away with my Italian leather shoe, and point at the phone in her hand.

"I, uhh, I think you should go." Her sultry voice cracks slightly, and worry glimmers in her honey orbs.

I scrub my palm across my jaw and give my head a shake. "You knew when you spoke those words to me downstairs in the snow who I was," I rumble. "You knew I'd been watching that woman, and you stopped me. You drew my focus on you. And instead of running away, you shook your ass, jabbered your nonsense, and showed me to your home. If that isn't a fucking invitation, I don't know what is."

She blinks at me, her tits jiggling with each frantic breath she takes. "Anyone ever tell you you're intense?" she asks as she texts someone on her phone.

I should worry she's contacting the police or her father or Olivia, whom I know lives two stories above them. Instead, she sends her text and tosses her phone into a chair nearby.

"You need a drink," she tells me as she turns and heads for the kitchen.

I prowl after her, shedding my long coat on the chair along the way. Inside the kitchen, I find her pouring some cheap vodka into two mismatched glasses. She hands me the one with *Beauty and the Beast* on the side, and I growl. This earns a snort from her.

"Do you have to stalk all your girlfriends? I mean, does anyone ever fall for this upon meeting them the first time? All growls and bossiness and . . ." She trails off and gestures at my suit. "And whatever this is."

"Tom Ford," I answer. "It cost more than your car."

She laughs, and it makes my heart rate speed up. "Something tells me you actually do know how much my car cost. But before you launch into a terrifying tale of how you managed to get that information in such a very short amount of time, please drink the vodka and chill out for a minute."

I knock back the horrendous alcohol and slam the glass back down on the counter. She shakes her head as though I, James Motherfucking Darden, amuse her.

I don't amuse anyone.

Her full, red lips hug the edge of the glittery glass she holds, and she daintily sips down the liquor that tastes worse than gasoline. She's not old enough to drink. But that doesn't matter because she's probably not old enough for the shit I plan to do to her.

Own. Possess. Destroy.

I want to tear her dress away with my teeth and bite every soft part of her. I want to rub my cock against her, letting my pre-cum leak onto her skin, and draw orgasm after orgasm from her simply from my tongue.

"When I want something, I take my time. This isn't something quick that will go away tomorrow, faster than a hangover from a twelve-dollar bottle of vodka." I stalk over to her and run my fingertip along her naked throat to her collarbone. Then, I dip it down to her cleavage. Her breath hitches, but she doesn't cower away. "This is something you will savor, girl. You'll savor it unlike anything you've ever had the pleasure of consuming. I will spoil you with my tongue, and you'll reward me with your cunt."

Her cheeks turn bright red, and for a moment, the usually jabbering girl is stunned silent. Those perfect fucking lips part in surprise. Those lips are my next victim. I go in for the kill without warning.

Tangling my large hands in her silky, wild-colored hair, I fist her locks on each side and tilt her head up. Her honey eyes are wide, but her mouth parts farther, inviting me in.

Too bad I don't wait for invitations.

I take what I want.

A mewl escapes her the moment my lips press firmly against hers. My tongue thrusts out to meet her small, unsure one, and I dominate her sexy little mouth. She's caught beneath a beast, this beauty, as I press my body against hers and lock her between me and the refrigerator.

Holding her hair isn't enough.

I am greedy.

My palm roves down along her jaw to her throat. With a swipe of my thumb over the fat vein in her neck, I revel in the way it pulses wildly. Anticipation and delight mixed in one extraordinary feeling. The fact that she is not afraid has my cock harder than stone.

"Your mouth, so young and supple, belongs to that of a woman. But you are simply a girl," I remind her. Warning her that I'm about to do grown-man things to her. "If ever there were a time to run, it would be now."

I pull away to stare at her perfect mouth that her breaths rush in and out of.

"But fair warning, Alice," I growl. "I'll chase you down any fucking rabbit hole. I'll always catch you."

CHAPTER FOUR

CERYS

MY MOUTH GAPES AT HIS OVERCONFIDENCE. There's something sexy and intriguing about it, but there's also a hint of annoyance that trickles through me. Those dark eyes bore into me. They dive deep into my being as if he's attempting to burrow through all the walls I've hidden behind.

Something tells me this man will rip me to shreds. Self-confidence has never been my strong suit. Hence the weird clothes and baggy sweaters. I hide behind the bright colors because I don't want people looking at me. But that's when they stare. Their eyes glued to the weird girl.

"This isn't a fairytale, Stalker Darden," I mutter, turning away from him. I lift the bottle, pouring another steep shot of the vile alcohol. His body cocoons me suddenly; heat on my back stifles me. I'm pinned between the counter and his broad, hard, yet lean body.

His hot breath fans over my neck, and his large hand grips my hair, tugging my head to the side. "Listen to me, Alice, I've devoured countless women. I've left them boneless," he murmurs. There's a promise in his words. He wants to do that to me. "Because I'm that fucking good." This time, his words are growled along my flesh, causing goosebumps to skitter wildly over every inch of my body. I can't stop trembling. He exudes a dominating presence. Commanding and extremely sexy.

Finally, he releases my hair, and I take the chance to spin on my heel. Meeting his eyes is something else. Something dark and feral glistens in them, stealing my breath and speeding up my heartbeat.

His gaze falls to my lips, trailing down to my nipples, which harden under his scrutiny. "Your tits are small," he utters.

"Perhaps your dick is small," I bite back in anger, but as soon as the words fall from my lips, I want to swallow them back. I shouldn't have said it. I know it's a lie, because how can a man like him be small?

That's when he turns rabid. He grips my throat, lifting me against the cabinet, pressing his groin against my stomach. I feel every rigid inch of him as he pushes against me, informing me wordlessly that he's loaded. There's a gun in there, and he will most certainly kill me with it.

"Is that small enough for you, Alice?" He chuckles, the sound vibrating through his chest against mine. He's close. Too fucking close.

His unique scent envelopes me. Coffee and whiskey, mingled with the sickly stench of the cheap vodka.

"You're an asshole," I choke out, his fingers tightening around my slim throat.

There's an animalistic grin on his handsome face as I claw at his neck. But the more I struggle, the harder he gets. I feel his cock throbbing against my abdomen. As if it has a pulse of its own.

"Listen to me, Alice—"

"Cerys. My name is Cerys," I breathe out when he releases me slightly. His grip still around my neck, but his hold isn't as tight.

"Cerys." He says my name slowly, as if tasting it on his tongue.

He leans in, ever so slightly. His full lips near mine. Involuntarily, my mouth opens for him, but he doesn't kiss me. My cheeks burn in shame for a moment before his tongue laps at the sensitive spot behind my ear. He pulls the lobe into his mouth, his teeth biting down on the flesh, causing me to whimper.

I shouldn't want this.

I shouldn't want him to hurt me.

But I do.

My thighs squeeze together. My hands land on his shoulders, gripping him, wanting to pull him closer.

"Why?" I whimper when he suckles the flesh.

He releases my neck, his hot mouth moving to the nape, planting kisses, suckling the skin, and biting so hard I know he's going to leave a bruise. He still hasn't answered me when his hands find the hem of my dress.

"Stop me," he growls a second before he lifts the material to my upper thighs. "If you don't want this, you best tell me right now."

I open my mouth.

I don't respond.

His fingers trail my inner thighs roughly. He kicks my one foot away, spreading my legs. I'm open to him. To his gaze and his ministrations. A soft mewl tumbles from my lips when he strokes my panties with two strong fingers. Again, and again. He continues to rub my pussy until I'm gripping his arms, digging my short nails into the material of his expensive suit, attempting to rip it from his body.

"Little Alice, falling down the rabbit hole," he murmurs in my ear before pulling away to regard me with a sinful smirk on his handsome face. "Let me take you to Wonderland." It's tempting, so fucking insanely tempting that I want to agree.

My head drops back when he pushes my panties to the side. Finding my drenched center, he continues to taunt me as he rubs against my needy flesh. It's slow, meticulous, just how I expected him to be. This man doesn't do things without thinking them through.

"You'll give in. You will submit because I won't stop until you do," he promises, causing me to snap my gaze to his. There's no lie in his eyes. I knew it.

We're at a standoff. He wants me to give in. I don't want to. But I don't want him to stop. I spread my legs farther, my hips rolling against his fingers.

"You're so filthy, Alice." He chuckles wolfishly. "Come for me. Use my fingers for your pleasure, little girl," he growls, his body rigid. He's barely holding onto his restraint. He teases my clit with his thumb while his other fingers slide against my opening, but never fully entering me. I cry out loudly, lost in the moment, as my body writhes in pleasure.

He doesn't stop.

"Please," I beg.

He rubs me harder, faster, pressing against my clit, causing my toes to curl. I see stars as my body convulses, the slick juices of my orgasm leaking from me and drenching his fingers.

"That's it, my dirty girl. Come for me. Come for your filthy stalker." His words wash over me as I leap from the edge into the darkness, and I cry out his name.

James. James. *James.*

CHAPTER FIVE

JAMES

"JAMES. JAMES. *JAMES*." MY NAME rolls off her sweet tongue like a chanted prayer. As though she's a forest nymph praying for the gods to shower their blessings upon her.

I'll be her god.

I'll shower her with pleasure until she's soaked to the bone and shivering for a reprieve.

"Ahh," she cries out, her body jolting

when a cute-as-fuck orgasm steals her from me. Her eyes roll back, and her back arches, a sultry moan tumbling past her lips. I rub her slowly and let her find her way back to reality one breath at a time.

I take a step back from her and bring my fingertips to my nose. Her scent is clean and sweet and fucking unlike anything I've smelled before. It makes my cock strain in my slacks. I need this woman like I need my next breath.

"Coat. Shoes. Now," I bark out. "We're leaving."

She blinks at me in confusion, still drunk from her orgasm. "Where will we go?"

On a slow ride to hell where I will taint

every pure cell of your body with the evil
sexual darkness that is me.

"My place."

Her answer is given to me by her amber eyes. A flaming desire burning like fire rages there, desperate for the hell my body promises hers. We don't need words. Stories can be told in silence.

Ours is steady breathing.

Narrowed, challenging eyes.

A fisting of my hand and a biting of her lip.

Silent yet powerful and predicting a future of unfiltered pleasure. I'll give it to her raw. Show her what it feels like to lose your mind and control together at once.

She flitters past me and disappears deeper into the apartment. I throw on my coat and wait impatiently at the door. Her farewell party waits with me, circling my feet like four demons supporting the devil in his nefarious plans for an angel.

And fuck . . . she is an angel.

Even in her stupid yellow coat.

Sunshine and warmth and youth and *mine*.

I hold my hand out to her, and she walks over to me, curious but wary. As she should be. I clasp her hand into mine and all but drag her through the building. We trek through the snow outside that's falling heavily now, but the flats she threw on are no match for the depth.

Too slow.

I need her to hurry the fuck up.

Bending down, I grab her by her waist and hoist the tiny thing over my shoulder. She lets out a loud, happy squeal that makes my black heart thrum to life. A devil has feelings, it would seem. She's cracked me right open and dug deep inside. I like her there.

I give her thighs a squeeze before I storm through the blistering wind and relentless snow. When I walk into my hotel, I bypass the front desk, ignoring all the stares, and head straight down the hall to my private elevator.

"It stopped snowing," she sasses. "Since we're inside and all. You can put me down."

Ignoring her, I enter the code to the elevator and step inside when it opens, my haul secured over my shoulder.

"Is this a normal thing for you?" she asks, her tone mildly irritated.

"What? Kidnapping bratty, beautiful girls who make poor fashion choices?" I ask and slap the back of her thighs with my palm. "Nope. First time, I must say."

"You're, like, the biggest freak I've ever met, and, like, I can't even be mad at you," she grumbles. "Believe me. I'm trying. But it's hard when you smell so good."

The doors open to my private suite, and my lips part too. A smile. She makes me fucking smile. I pack that thought away for later. Not much in this life brings me joy. Pleasure? Yes. Joy? Never.

But Cerys Youngblood, crazy girl with crazy hair and an abhorrent affection for disgusting liquor and demon cats?

Most definitely.

"The floors are amazing," she says in a dry tone. "Prettiest floors I've ever seen. I wonder what the rest of the place looks like."

I lower her to her feet but keep my grip around her sweet curves in a tight hold. "Pretty sure when my tongue is inside you in a few minutes, you won't give a goddamn about the floors."

She tilts her head up and regards me with a soft, tender expression I don't like. It makes my mind contract and expand. Like she's pulling some sort of wicked sorcery and planting thoughts inside me.

Scary thoughts.

Evil, evil thoughts.

Like thoughts where she still looks up at me that same way for years to come.

Fucking years.

She's sentencing me to a future, and I've barely met this warden.

"I'm going to come out with it, Stalker Darden," she says with a huff. "I have small boobs which you already pointed out. And with small, disappointing boobs comes disappointing virgins."

I blink at her. "And your point?"

"My point is, I'm not some sex goddess you probably think I am. I mean, I talk a good talk and all, but—"

My mouth crashes to hers, and she lets out a surprised moan. I grab her tight ass and carry her down the hallway. I flip on the lights to my bedroom and carry her over to my massive bed. It doesn't see much action besides sleeping. The fucks I do allow myself happen elsewhere. This is my safe haven. The only fucking place I can relax.

So why did you bring her here?

My maddening thoughts mock me.

Because she's sunshine and warmth and a Corona on the motherfucking beach.

I lay her down on the bed and revel in

the nervous way she stares up at me. I'm desperate to maul her, but she's putting so much trust in a monster, I can't help but bow and yield to her. Perhaps another time I will destroy her. For now, I'll spread her legs and lap at her cunt, a submissive beast.

"Take off your coat and dress," I order, my voice sharp and demanding as I yank at my tie.

Her fingers shake, but she obeys me. Sweet girl. She tosses her clothing away and sits there looking cute as fuck in her mismatched bra and panties. Red bra. Pink panties. Fucking awful, and yet I find it the most adorable damn thing I've ever seen. Nonetheless, I want them gone.

"Bare, Cerys. Now." I yank off my coat and then suit jacket before throwing them into a chair.

Her cheeks blaze pink, but she removes her undergarments. When I pluck through the buttons of my shirt, her honey eyes track the movement. I slide away the material and yank off my undershirt as well. The tiny mewl that escapes her reminds me of her demon cats. This little kitten wants to lick me too.

"Show me your cunt, girl," I growl.

She bites on her bottom lip and slowly parts her thighs. Too slow. I grip her knees as I drop to one of mine and part her open. She's bare. Fuck, that's hot. Her pussy lips are pink, and her opening glistens with her arousal.

I'm going to destroy this.

Ruin it with every part of me.

I've never been so delighted in all my life.

My mouth is a beast of its own as I seek out her sweet taste. The moment my tongue laps at her arousal, she cries out, her fingers latching onto my hair.

Pulling and guiding and grumbling out orders.

She's a beast, too, it would seem.

I suck on her clit, brutally so, and enjoy the scream of pleasure mixed with pain that has her arching off the bed. My finger dips slightly into her opening, seeing how tight she really is, and I am pleased to discover her body responds so easily to me.

Tugging at her outer lips of her pussy with my teeth, I inch my finger deeper into her heat, loving the slurping sounds her body is making.

"Little girl?"

"Y-Yes?"

"You can scream all you want. They won't hear you."

CHAPTER SIX

CERYS

HIS MOUTH IS MAGIC.

He's a magician, and he's toying with me, working me into a frenzy. His tongue darts between my wet folds, tasting, licking, devouring. I've never been eaten out, but the way his mouth teases, taunts, and sucks on the smooth lips of my pussy, I know he's had far too much experience.

Shutting my eyes, I try not to think about the number of women he's probably brought here. Or about how many have been right in this position. My thighs squeeze around his head as he barely teases two fingers into me. He doesn't go farther than his second knuckle. He could, but then he'd be drenched in my virginity.

My thoughts are scattered between the moans he elicits from me and the fear that this is my first time and I'm about to do it with a man who's old enough to be my father.

"Fuck," he growls, causing my eyes to snap open. I regard him with wild, hungry eyes. I'm needy. I'm so close, so near orgasm that all I need is a tiny push. Something that will take the edge off, but he doesn't give it to me.

"Please, Stalker," I taunt him sounding breathy when I utter the words.

"You'll come on my tongue," he orders. "I want all those juices drenching me. Your cunt is so tight, little girl." He smirks this time, a feral expression on his face.

I'm about to respond when he drops his mouth to my core and continues to lick at me, gently fingering me, taunting my clit, biting down hard then suckling gently. The back and forth sensations turning me inside out, and I know that's his mission.

"Oh, fuck, fuck," I curse, my voice a shrill scream when he finally allows me an orgasm by swirling his tongue, fingers, and mouth on my pussy. I'm over the edge of bliss when I feel another finger at my other entrance.

"Mmmm," James moans as he drinks in my arousal like it's his sustenance and he's been starving for months, years even. My body relinquishes everything to him. All control is his. He knew he'd steal it from me. He was confident in his ministrations.

When I open my eyes again, I find him staring up at me. He doesn't have to say anything at all. He knows he's won.

"You're an evil bastard," I bite out as he pulls his fingers away from me.

He rises, shoving his boxers down his impossibly thick, muscled thighs. For an older man, he's sexy, not chiseled like those young guys you see on magazines, but rather toned and solid. It makes me want him even more.

"Have you ever sucked a cock?" he says, his tone filled with amusement at me openly gawking at the angry erection jutting out from between his thighs. The man is huge. There's glistening arousal on the tip, leaking for me.

For me.

"No," I tell him honestly, gazing up at him. "I'm embarrassed to say this is the first ever penis I've seen in real life."

He chuckles at my confession. "Well, take a good long look, because soon, this will be down your pretty little throat," he promises.

"What?"

"On your knees," he orders, and I

immediately find myself falling to the soft, plush carpet. It's fluffy and warm, and I settle in because I know this is going to be a long night. He steps closer to me and continues with his directions. "Take it in your hand, stroke it up and down, slowly."

I obey. My hand looks tiny attempting to wrap around the thickness of his shaft. It's warm and silky to the touch, and it jolts when I come into contact with it.

"Lick it."

I move forward, my tongue darting out as I tentatively lap at the salty liquid on the tip. It's musky, but with a salty sweetness swirled together, reminding me of a salted caramel treat. My lips wrap around the head, taking him into my mouth like I've seen on those videos online. My eyes dart up to find him watching me in awe as I swallow his length.

I move slowly, his hands fist my hair, holding me steady as he guides himself into my warm, wet mouth. His hips move back and forth, gently at first, but with every inch he pushes into me, he speeds up.

When his cock hits the back of my throat, I gag, spluttering and choking around the thickness. "That's it," he mumbles, his eyes glued to mine. "Take me, deeper, little girl," he grunts. His cock throbs, causing me to choke. Tears sting my eyes and saliva drips from my chin, but he smiles. "So, fucking beautiful when you cry and choke," he praises, fucking my mouth like he would my body, my pussy, and I know he'll do it to my ass as well.

He moves faster, my hands reach for his thighs, attempting to hold him back, but I can't. I'm nowhere near strong enough. Fear dances in my mind, in my chest, and I know when he shakes his head, he sees it in my eyes.

"Calm, little one," he tells me, but doesn't relent. "Just take it. Touch your pretty pussy for me," he orders, and I obey him easily.

My one hand finds my core drenched with arousal. I stroke myself, causing a whimper to vibrate in my throat, which in turn causes him to growl and shudder. I do it again, watching in awe as this man who seems to always be in control slowly falls apart in my mouth.

I reach for his balls, cupping them as I breathe through the way he slides into my throat, and deep-throat for the first time in my life, shocking the shit out of me and him.

One last moan from me, and James stills. I think I've done something wrong, but then I feel it. Jet after jet of hot cum spills into my throat, and I can't help but smile.

One point for me, Stalker.

CHAPTER SEVEN

JAMES

SHE'S BEAUTIFUL.

Too beautiful.

The thought is alarming, and possessive thoughts thrash at the surface of my mind.

Keep her. Keep her. Fucking keep her.

She slides her mouth off my cock and flashes me a smug smile. For her first blow job, she knows she nailed it. And I'm going to nail *her*.

But first . . .

"Are you hungry?"

Her brows furrow in confusion. "What?"

"Food, Cerys. Humans eat it. Want some?" I smirk at her as I offer her my hand.

She stands, and her small tits bounce with the movement. The girl thinks they're something to be ashamed of. When I made a comment about the size, it wasn't because I didn't like them. It was simply stating a fact. They're perfect. Little bite-sized nibbles of sweetness.

"Um, I thought . . ." She trails off and crosses her arms over her lovely breasts.

"Don't worry, love," I assure her. "I'm going to fuck you. But I told you I was going to savor you. If I were to pounce on you now and take that sweet virginity, it'd be over in a flash. I'd like to share a meal with you."

She blinks at me as though I've lost my mind. I yank one of my T-shirts from my drawer and toss it at her. Then I slide on some sweatpants before calling room service. I order my favorites and then hang up.

She's quiet but certainly curious. Her fingers flit along my furniture as she inspects decorations and framed photographs and art on the walls. "This is beautiful," she tells me, pointing a slender finger at the wall.

"I bought it last summer in Venice. A small gallery off the beaten path. The person who painted this was blind. He wasn't always that way, but an accident ruined his eyesight.

His paintings are his way of converting what he still sees in his mind onto a blank canvas. Through his paintings, we see what we think he cannot see." I close my eyes as I wrap my arms around her from behind. Her scent is mixed with mine, and I fucking love it. "I could recall every detail about you. I'd never need my eyes again, Cerys. You've burned yourself into my brain."

"For how long? How long do you keep us? You were after Liv. I'm sure you pursue women often, because look at you. So how long will this go on for?" Her body is tense in my arms.

Gripping her hips through the thin material of my shirt, I twist her and press my body against hers, locking her against the wall. "I never keep them. They are for my momentary enjoyment. I get bored easily."

She rolls her eyes and lets out a huff. "Maybe this was a mistake. I don't know . . . I thought maybe this thing between us was intense and possibly lasting?"

Her innocence is a decadent treat dripping with need and the desire to be adored. I want to devour it whole.

"I've never been so utterly obsessed by someone upon meeting them." I gently clutch her throat as my eyes bore into hers. "I'm not sure I'll ever let you leave this room."

She giggles, but I'm completely serious.

Her red-and-black hair. Her honey eyes.

Her tiny tits and smooth-shaven cunt. It all looks really fucking good in my room. Like it belongs. And not like a fleeting thought, but like a memory etched in time and painted on a canvas that remains a permanent fixture on the wall.

I'm keeping her.

The buzzer rings, and I reluctantly pull away from her. Stalking through my home, I make my way to the door. A man with a cart pushes inside. He nods at me, and then he's gone. Cerys bounces up beside me and starts lifting lids. I'm amused at her excitement over food. Stepping back, I let her dip and taste and babble on about how "oh my God, this is amazing" the foods are. I push the cart over to the table and unload it all. She sits on the edge of the table and eats right from the plate using her fingers, bypassing utensils altogether. Normally, this sort of rash behavior would unnerve me, but she distracts me. Blinds me in her dazzling beauty and ease.

"I'm not the type of girl to run off with a madman and do"—she waves her hand in the air— "this, you know?"

"This?" I implore, no longer hungry for food. I'm hungry for her plump lips and hard, little pink nipples poking through the fabric of the shirt.

"Careless, whatever this is."

I watch her with narrowed eyes until I'm

sure she's had plenty to eat. Then, I grab her wrist and pull her off the table.

"Time to do more careless things, love."

She laughs, but it's nervous in nature. Once I get her naked again, her nerves won't matter. Orgasms will matter.

When we're back in my room, I practically rip my shirt in two trying to rid her of it. My sweatpants get lost next, and then I slide an arm around her narrow waist. I pick her up with my achingly hard cock between us and carry her to the bed. Together we go down. Her eyes are wide, and her fingernails dig into my shoulders as though she's ready to draw blood if need be. I situate myself between her narrow thighs and rest my cock against her smooth cunt.

"Are you scared?" I murmur, my nose inches from hers.

She swallows and gives me a slight nod. "Kinda."

"Scared I'll hurt you?"

"In more ways than you know."

"A little pain can be nice though," I tell her. "A little pain makes you appreciate the pleasure. It's a reminder that not everything is sweet."

"I'm afraid . . ." She trails off and turns her head.

I grip her jaw and move her head until our eyes lock once again. "Afraid of my fat cock stretching you and making you bleed?"

I arch a brow in question.

"More like afraid of you ripping my heart out and feeding on it," she admits with a whisper.

I rub my cock between the lips of her pussy against her clit. "I don't care about hearts," I tell her with a frown. "Why would I want that?"

She blinks at me sadly. "Exactly."

"I'm not a normal man," I admit, my hips unrelenting as they rock against her.

"No shit?" she deadpans, her voice breathy.

"I don't feel or think as one should. I'm not a romantic or even sweet." Guilt surges up inside of me, and I hate the feeling. "If that is what you're looking for . . ."

She laughs. "I wasn't looking for anything. It found me, remember?"

Despite her laughter, her eyes are sad. Lonely. Longing and aching for connection. I've seen the despondent look in my own reflection at times. I don't understand it, but I feel allured by it.

Her eyes dart past me toward the door, and I frantically think she might just up and leave. The thought is maddening, and it has me gripping her wrists to pin her to the bed. Wild amber eyes lock with mine, and her lips part. I rub and rub and rub my cock against her clit until she's whimpering out another breathy orgasm. The condoms are in the drawer. So close.

"I need to put on a condom," I bark out, irrationally angry at her for putting me under her spell.

"So do it."

I pull away slightly and look between us. She looks too. My tip presses gently into her, barely so, much like my fingers from before.

"This is dangerous," I warn.

"You're dangerous," she bites back.

Our eyes clash again. She is fiery and brave and curious and so goddamned trusting. If you bare your throat to a beast, he's going to bite it. He's going to exert his power over you.

"I could fuck you bare, girl. What do you

think about that?"

Her challenging eyes narrow, and her nostrils flare. "I think you talk a lot."

With a growl and a hard thrust of my hips, I drive into the tightest fucking cunt I've ever been inside of. Her screams—*my God, how they're loud*—rival that of the roars of my own beastliness. She has claws. Fuck, how she has claws. And she uses them. Tears at the flesh of my arms as I drive into her again.

She's driven me to madness.

I'm not myself in this woman's presence.

I'm not wild and free.

She has caged me.

It is me who bares his throat and she who stakes claim over me.

My, how the roles have reversed.

"James," she utters, two tears leaking out of the corner of each of her eyes.

Leaning forward, I dart my tongue out and lick one of them from her temple. "I know, Cerys. I feel it too."

CHAPTER EIGHT

CERYS

MY BODY ARCHES AS HE MOVES INSIDE me, thickening, stretching me painfully. As much as I should feel scared, I don't. He holds me so close. He moves in sync with me, as if I'd been made for him. To offer him pleasure as he draws it from me.

I cry out with every thrust. He doesn't make love to me; he fucks me. He's a beast, hungry and feral. An animal taking what he needs, and I revel in it. Our gazes lock as he continues to open me, connecting not only our bodies, but something deeper I can't explain.

I can't help wincing as he rolls his hips, bucking into me like a man possessed. There's pleasure and pain rippling through me, and it feels as if I can't root myself to just one emotion. Torn, weather-beaten by a man who was a stranger, but now . . . now he's here, taking my virginity, and I want him to.

"You're an animal," I whimper, clawing his skin with my nails, causing his face to light up with satisfaction. He wants me to hurt him the same way he hurts me. I lift my hips, clenching my pussy until he's growling like a bear.

There's an ache in my chest threatening

to burst, and my eyes leak with salty emotion. He feels it too. His eyes bore into mine, watching me as I come apart beneath him. His body, so large and heavy, fucks me into the mattress.

He leans in, licking the tears from my face, savoring my taste. "Wet my dick, little girl," he murmurs against my lips. Stealing one between his teeth, he bears down, biting hard. I whimper as it shoots a jolt of electricity straight to my clit, and I fly over the edge.

My slick walls pulse around his length, and he grunts, causing his chest to vibrate against mine. His body locks suddenly, and I half expect him to pull out, but he doesn't. Heat fills me, thick and fast, and I know there's no going back now.

He's just marked me from the inside out.

His mouth latches onto my small breast as he sucks my pink bud hard, biting it until I cry out, and another wave rushes over me. When I glance down, there's a slight pink bruise on the porcelain skin of my tit.

"You're mine now, little girl."

I meet his eyes but can't find words to respond.

I want this man.

I need him to claim me.

To give me everything I hunger for. To offer me the affection I so clearly crave. My heart thuds as my nails rake down his back. He drives into me, and I feel him soften as he continues to tease my sore pussy.

He regards me as if I'm one of his expensive paintings, with awe and wonderment. A gentle touch to my cheek ignites the ache in my chest once more. It's a tender moment, one you'd expect from a long-term lover, not a man who'd just fucked you until you're broken and boneless.

"I—I don't know what this means," I croak, my throat thick with emotion holding my voice hostage.

"What are you doing to me?" he asks, pained and tormented. There's an honesty in his tone, a brokenness that makes him seem more fragile than I am.

I reach for his face, cupping his cheek in

my small palm, reveling in the rough feeling of his stubble as it tickles my hand. "Are you scared of me?"

My question jars him, causing him to pull out of my body abruptly, eliciting a painful mewl from my lips. He slides off the bed, his back muscles tensing with the quick movement.

"Shit," he curses, stalking back and forth around the room, his fingers tangling in his hair. His softened cock is stained crimson with my virginity mixed with arousal. The scent of us in the air is heavy, like a perfume I want to hold onto forever.

Forever.

What the fuck is wrong with me?

I'm not some stupid teenage girl who does this. But I've just done it. I've just offered myself like a sacrifice to Lucifer himself, and the man who's now standing before me is at war with himself. Does he regret what we did? Is he going to throw me out now?

"I—I . . . I'm sorry," I mumble, pushing off the bed quickly, not realizing my body is still coming down from the most intense orgasms I've ever experienced. My knees give out, and I brace myself for the impact with the carpet. But he's there, my beast, pulling me into his arms.

"You need to lie down, love," he tells me, his voice gentle and caring. A vast difference from the violent way he swore only moments ago. As if there are two people living inside his head, he leaps from one to the other within a matter of seconds.

I obey him and my heart rate picks up when he kneels on the bed at my feet.

"You're not kicking me out now?" I question innocently, ignoring the fact that his fingers are stroking my hips, thighs, and slowly spreading my legs once more. He doesn't look in my eyes. His gaze is glued to my pussy.

"I could never throw you out," he confesses quietly, flitting his stare to mine, which is drenched in guilt. "I've marked you," he decrees. "You're mine. Do you understand that?"

"But—"

"Cerys, I want to keep you. Tell me I can keep you." His words sound pained. As if he's the one cracking beneath the weight of this emotion stealing us from the outer world. I want to be here, inside this hotel room, but I have a life to think of—school, my Dad, who would have a fit if he knew what I just did.

"How is this going to work?" My voice is timid, scared of what my heart is doing, what it's wanting.

James doesn't respond. Instead, he leans in, planting soft kisses on my inner thighs. He runs his nose along the smooth skin, causing goosebumps to dot my flesh. When he reaches the apex between my legs, he inhales me as if

I'm a perfume. A fresh flower to be plucked from the wild, hidden in a glass cage for him to admire.

"James," I whimper when he slowly laps at my core. Everything south of my belly button tightens, coils like a serpent ready to attack, but I can't move because his hands have my hips pinned to his large bed.

He continues to lick and nibble on my bare lips, suckling on my clit. His teeth bite down, sending sparks through my veins, heating my blood once more.

"We . . . We . . . Oh God," I cry out when he eases two fingers deep into me. The sounds my body makes from the juices dripping down to my ass makes me blush as he takes me higher and higher with every movement.

Pleasure grips me, and I fist the blanket below me to keep from tearing his hair out to pull him closer. My toes curl when he releases my hips to taunt my pussy and my ass. One finger teases the tight hole, which makes me tense.

"Breathe, sweetheart," he murmurs against my flesh. "I'm not taking this hole tonight, but soon my fat cock will stretch it wide." There's no doubt in his tone. His ministrations turn me into a molten puddle as he works my body like a fine-tuned instrument, and I'm flying apart in seconds as I'm filled in both holes by his expert fingers.

As I come down from the high, James

moves from between my legs to spoon behind me. His thick cock pressed between my thighs, his arm wrapped around me possessively, and I can't help but melt into the heat of him.

"Sleep now, little girl. Tomorrow we'll talk," he whispers as my heavy eyelids fall closed.

CHAPTER NINE

JAMES

I PACE IN FRONT OF THE WINDOWS, CONFUSED and overwhelmed. My entire home is saturated in her scent, and she's barely been here eight hours. While she fell right to sleep last night, I laid awake thinking about everything.

And I do mean everything.

My brain is a maddening mess of thoughts.

No stone gets unturned.

I contemplate every possible outcome of my perfect problem sleeping in my bed. She's most definitely a problem though. Little, beautiful, no-longer-a-virgin Cerys has infected my mind. It was a weak place to begin with. Slivered and cracked from an abusive childhood. A small child can only take so many beat downs by vile adults before they start retreating into themselves. Before they start imagining new realities for themselves. Before they start planning futures that may never exist. By the time I turned eighteen and hit the ground running, my mind was already fragmented into a not-so-beautiful kaleidoscope of insanity. It's taken everything in me to keep it all on a tight leash. And admittedly, the past year, it's been running away from me like an abused animal who can't stand his owner. The irony is not lost on me.

But now?

Now, the madness is off the leash and running rampant.

Gone. Gone. Gone.

I have a meeting with an Italian businessman later this morning, and I can't find it in me to care. It's the biggest potential deal in my entire career. If he wants to sell me a beautiful piece of property in Venice, Darden Hotels could be looking to expand there in the near future. It's a dream come true.

And yet . . .

My dreams are fuzzy clouds of nothingness.

A fog of pretend.

Something a child dreams up.

Reality snores—*yes, she snores*—in the other room, and for once, I want to stay rooted in the moment. Live in the realness of life and not the possibilities. But with living in the present and not focusing solely on what's out in front of me, who the fuck am I anymore? James Darden is a conqueror. A planner. A goal smasher. James Darden reaches for what he can't have and he makes it his.

Always reaching and reaching and reaching.

What happens when I have it in my grasp?

I don't know what to fucking do with it, that's what.

The toilet flushes in the other room, and I freeze. My gaze is locked outside where I can stare straight ahead at the building across the street. Above where I've figured is Cerys's apartment, the curtains are pulled open, and Olivia prances around looking blonde and tall and uninteresting. I'm baffled how in less than twenty-four hours I can go from obsessing over taking that woman out to fucking the virginity out of her future stepdaughter.

I'll get bored of Cerys.

The thought causes an ache to form in

my chest.

Right?

I get bored of everything.

It's an inevitability. A known future. Storms of feelings that will eventually break land and obliterate us both.

I'm doing this.

Me.

Ruining it all because I can. Because I will. Because it's the Darden way.

"You're probably not even mine," he *sneers. "Your mother always was a whore."*

The voice, so harsh and cruel from my past, leaves me shaking and my heart racing.

Not real. Not real. Not real.

My past sometimes haunts me when I'm

feeling stressed out. Right now, I'm feeling really fucking stressed out.

"Hey," a sweet voice croaks, shoving all hateful ghosts back into their box and slamming the lid closed. "I wondered where you went."

I turn my laser-sharp focus on her and track her with my intense stare. She's put back on her black dress, but her messy hair is a fright. My fingers twitch to force her to kneel before me so I can run my fingers through each tangle and smooth them out for her. Instead, I fist my hands.

I'll break her.

I'll break her heart so it matches my mind.

I'm going to do it, and I can't stop myself.

"Hey," I reply, my voice harsh and hateful, not unlike the one of my father. My chest aches further to the point I don't know how much more I can take.

"I could make you breakfast," she squeaks out, nervously biting on her bottom lip.

She's a gorgeous mess. I should have stayed in bed. I should have carried her into the shower with me. I should have claimed her again and again and again.

"I don't eat breakfast."

She winces at my words and looks past me at the heavily falling snow. "Okay," she breathes out and walks over to the windows.

"Would you like to come over and have lunch later? I make a mean grilled cheese."

Yes, Cerys. I would love to have a motherfucking grilled cheese.

"I have a meeting," I bark out.

Her chin lifts, and she points at the windows where Olivia chatters on her cell phone. "What a great view," she says softly, all sarcasm gone.

Where did you go, Cerys?

Did I accidentally shove you into the box too?

I rub at the tension on the back of my neck and let out a heavy sigh. "I'll have one of the bellhops see to it that you make it home okay."

She jerks her head my way and regards me with watery eyes. "Just like that, huh?"

My nostrils flare because her scent is intoxicating. It makes me want to forget my responsibilities, let down my guard, and slide into bed with her. Take the time to stroke the tangles from her hair. Take all day to remind her how beautiful and funny and interesting she is to me.

"Not all of us are children who live with their daddies. Some of us have work to do." I close my eyes, hating how my words sound. I'm cruel. Just like him.

When I reopen my eyes, she's gone. Seconds later, she has her coat and shoes on. As she retreats in her yellow coat and messy hair, I can't help but follow. I wonder if it'll always be this way. She's running away from me because I'm a fucking psycho and me following because I'm a fucking psycho.

She turns the knob, but I slam my hand on the door above her and lean my body against hers. I inhale her hair and run my fingers through the ends.

"Cerys," I murmur, begging for her to find me in my inner darkness and shine a goddamned light on me. God, how I need her light.

"I'm leaving." Her voice cracks, and I can hear the emotion in it.

Suddenly, panicked and fearful of her not within my sight, I clutch onto her hips.

I nuzzle my nose in her hair and nip at her shoulder through the strands. She lets out a surprised gasp, and then laments, "James."

So desperate, like the way my head is chanting her name on repeat in my head.

So sad.

"I'm a fucked-up man." That's my only explanation. It's the only bone I've ever offered anyone. I don't know how to explain myself. This is me trying with every fiber of my being to do so. I can feel her slipping from me, and I don't know what to do.

"No shit?" Her sarcastic, almost amused tone, has me eager to rekindle what we had last night.

I slide an arm around her waist and haul

her over to the couch. The need to have this woman—to show her with my body how much I physically need her—is overpowering.

"I don't understand you," she proclaims, her voice tearful and confused. "I don't understand you, James."

Hell, I don't understand me.

"I know," I grind out. "I'm sorry." I am, but I don't know what to do about it.

I bend her over the back of the couch and shove her dress up. Her panties get yanked down her thighs as I simultaneously free my cock from my slacks. I slap at her cunt from behind with my cock, and I can tell she's not wet for me. Gently, I finger her sensitive clit. I hardly know her, but I already know exactly what her body likes. As though my fingers were created to pleasure this part of her. And much to my delight, she rocks her hips and gives me the sounds that indicate she's enjoying my touches. It doesn't take long before her legs are quivering and she's crying out my name.

James.

It crawls from her lips like a question.

As though she's asking, "Why are we doing this? What are we doing?"

I have no answers because I don't know. I just know I need her more than anything I've ever needed. Gripping my throbbing cock, I slide the tip along her now wet entrance and drive all the way into her with one quick thrust. She screams—fuck, I know she's still sore—and fists the cushions on the couch.

"Tell me to stop," I choke out. *Tell me to be a better man.*

But she does nothing of the sort.

"Please," she begs. So many words hang thick in the air. She wants more than a brutal fucking over a couch.

She wants everything.

And I don't know how to give it to her.

I fist her dress in one hand under her coat and dig my fingers into her fleshy hip with the other. Pound after pound, I try to fuck into her my feelings. My thoughts. My desires. But wordless proclamations mean nothing.

"Cerys," I hiss.

Fuck. Fuck. Fuck.

She's driven me to utter insanity.

There's no coming back.

"I know," she sobs. "I feel it too."

With her sad words, I groan out my release. I can't be the man she needs. I'll never be. Which is exactly why I need to get my dick out of her fertile cunt. But I can't. I drain myself inside of her. Wishing and hoping and praying for futures I'll never have. And when I've had her completely, I pull out and stagger away.

On shaky legs, she stands and turns her teary eyes my way. I stuff my wet cock back into my slacks as she pulls her panties back up into place. Her eyes plead with mine. Beg me to crawl out of my head and into her arms.

"I could cook you dinner," she murmurs, her last attempt to save me from myself.

I reach my hand forward. My fisted hand because I'm so fucking furious at what an asshole I am. She grips my fist and kisses my middle knuckle. Her fingers uncurl my own and guide me to cup her jaw.

"James, say yes," she pleads, her tears leaking out and soaking my flesh.

My thumb swipes one of her tears. "We'll see."

She swallows and nods.

I watch her leave, and this time, I don't follow.

"I want you to cook me all my meals," I

mutter long after she's gone from my home. "Even breakfast. I'd eat breakfast for you."

Turning, I wait for her. Soon, in the middle of the snowstorm, a flash of yellow dances across the street. And before she walks into her building, she turns to look up. I doubt she can even see me from down there. Regardless, I palm the glass with one hand and rest my forehead to it.

"I want you to come back. I want you to stay."

But my words go unheard.

CHAPTER
TEN

CERYS

S SOON AS I STEP INSIDE THE APARTMENT, I shrug off my drenched coat, hanging it against the door to dry. Shoving off my shoes, I leave them at the entrance. Silence greets me. It's more stifling today than it ever was before. Dad isn't home. Nobody is here for me to come home to.

For five years since Mom died, he's been gone. Hidden away in his office or in Olivia's bed. He gave up on me a long time ago. But it's not that which now causes tears to sting my eyes. No, this time it's the man across the street.

James.

Even his name sends a pain so acute straight to my heart. As if a needle is prodding at the thudding muscle in my chest. Swallowing the emotion balled up in my throat, I pad over to the kitchen. Opening the fridge, I stare at the contents.

My mind flits back to moments ago when I looked into his eyes, seeing the agony so clear in his gaze only solidified my want of him. I want to fix him. It's impossible to change someone. There's no guarantee that once they're healed they'll stay with you, but something shifted between us last night.

Strange how you can meet someone who burrows their way into your very soul in one night. It wasn't the sex, which at first I believed it was. No. It was so much more than that.

His touch, the way he spoke to me, one moment he was wide open, a gaping abyss of melancholy and guilt, and the next, he would close up shop as if it's five p.m. on a Friday afternoon.

If I'd only found him earlier, a few seconds would've made a difference. Maybe I could've spoken to him. Made him see I wanted to be there.

The shrill ring of my mobile startles me

from my thoughts, and I shut the silver door of the refrigerator I still had open. With a quick glance at my screen, I notice it's my best friend.

The problem with speaking to her is she'll know something happened. We've been friends for almost ten years. Saskia has been beside me through everything from braces to my first crush on the most popular boy in school.

All of that was welcome. It was the growing pains most girls go through, but this . . . this is vastly different. I had sex with a man old enough to be my father. A man who's so broken he can't even ask me to stay and have breakfast with him.

His mood swings gave me whiplash. Back and forth.

When the ringing stops, I sigh a breath of relief, but it's short lived. I knew she wouldn't give up. I answer after the fifth ring. "Hey, Kia, what's up?" I attempt a smile, but it's forced. My voice is rigid with emotion.

"What's wrong, chickadee?" she asks playfully, but there's no humor coming from my end. "Oh no, what happened? Is it your dad? Did he finally propose to Cruella? Oh my God, don't tell me you finally found out that hipster clothes are so last season?" She sasses me with a snort and giggle.

"No," I sigh. "I think . . . I mean, I don't know, but I met someone."

"What?" Her screech is loud enough to wake all the damn cats in the neighborhood. "How am I only hearing about this now?"

"Calm down. I just got home."

"Oh, my fucking God, did you fuck him? Is his cock big?" she gasps down the line, causing me to laugh out loud. This is why she's my best friend. As painful as it is to think about how I walked out on him, I'm smiling because I'm happy. When I think about how much pleasure he gave me, my heart fills with emotion.

"He's older," I whisper, lowering my voice, but I don't see the point since I'm alone. There's something taboo about it, which only serves to send a tingle racing through me.

"Tell me everything, and I mean every-fucking-thing," Saskia orders.

"Ugh, fine," I respond, flopping onto the sofa, pulling my legs up and my feet under my ass. "Well, he owns the hotel chain Darden Hotels," I start, recalling everything that happened last night. And when I say I recall everything, I mean each tiny detail. "He was so loving, so rough, but gentle. He made me orgasm more times than I can count, and I mean, like, the real thing," I hiss down the line, blushing at my own words, at the memory of how my body responded to his.

"And then what happened this morning?"

"Well, that's the thing, he's . . ." I sigh, not knowing what to make of James Darden.

He's what? Broken? Hurt? Just an asshole? No. He's not an asshole, at least not all the time. But there's something he's hiding from me. I didn't expect us to confess our life stories, but I wanted more. Just a tad bit more.

"Will you see him again? I mean, you said he felt something too?" My best friend is always optimistic. Which in turn has me wondering if I should be like that too. Will I see him again? I don't know.

"Well, I did invite him for dinner, but I doubt I'll be hearing from him. I mean, it wasn't a date. He didn't say yes." The sadness in my voice is loud and clear. My heart thudded against my ribs when I asked him, when I took the leap into the unknown. But of course, he seemed unsure of what to do. Perhaps that's all we had, one night of bliss, and now I'm shoved out into the cold again.

"Listen to me, chickadee," my best friend advises. "Men are assholes, there's no doubt about that, but when they get a taste of some good pussy, there's no way they'll pass up the chance for a second taste," she informs me as if she's the parent educating me on romance and boys. Sometimes Saskia is older than me in that respect, but everywhere else, money and education, I'm the one who schools her.

"Do you have to be so vulgar?" I groan, recalling the dirty words James uttered to me. Each and every one of them made me wet and needy. Craving his touch, I dove in head first, not caring about the consequences.

"Come on, Cerys, don't tell me he didn't get vulgar with you." She giggles then, causing me to follow suit.

"Well . . ." My words taper off, knowing she's right.

"I knew it!" She sounds more excited than I feel. Perhaps I should paint and take my mind off the man from across the road. "Listen to me," she says, sounding serious for a moment. "He'll come around tonight. Just you wait." I nod even though she can't see me. Maybe she's right, but I'm not holding on to hope again, only to be let down. The one man in my life who always lets me down is Dad. I don't need another one.

"I guess. Listen, I'm spending the day inside. It's way too cold to go shopping."

"That's fine. Daddy dearest has his business associates over for lunch, and I'm playing hostess." Something in her tone hints at an underlying plan.

"Tell me more," I encourage, knowing my friend does not do things like this for no reason. At least, not for her father's benefit.

"Ha, fine. Daddy's new junior associate at the office is thirty-eight, but he's utterly delectable. He has those dark, brooding features, sorta like Justin Theroux. You know who I mean, Jennifer Aniston's hubs."

"Yeah, the dark and dangerous look. You do realize the dude is probably a psycho?"

"A hot psycho! Later, chickadee, and listen to me. He'll be over there. Just don't get that little heart into the mix. I don't want to have to go on a killing spree. Orange is not my best color. Love you, babe," she chatters, hanging up before I can get a word in. Dropping my phone on the sofa, I head into my studio and quickly change into my painting clothes. A low-cut, white tank top splattered with paint from years of use and small, cut-off shorts also multi-colored from different paints.

A loud banging on the door causes me to leap from the small wooden stool, dropping my palette paint-side onto the white cloth I placed down in case of an accident. Fuck.

I lean down to pick it up when another loud thud on the door has me jolting up. Someone's trying to break in. My heart pounds against my chest, leaping into my throat when I hear a click. They're trying to get into the apartment.

Thinking quick, I grab the paint thinner and race into the living room. I'm about to pull the door open when a voice comes from the other side.

"Open the fucking door, love." His rough, deep growl vibrates through the wood and through me too. Shit!

I cast a quick glance at my clothes, then

in the mirror in the hallway. I'm a mess. A fucking colorful mess. But if this is what he wants, he'll have to live with it. I pull open the door, and there, looking disheveled in another one of those expensive-ass suits, is the man who's been on my mind all day.

James Darden.

"What are you doing here?"

He doesn't respond, instead pushing through the door, knocking the bottle of paint thinner all over my shirt. His gaze is wild, panicked. It roves over me, from my messy black-and-red locks to my bare feet I notice have tiny pinpricks of yellow paint on them.

Immediately, Hank is around his ankles, twirling against the fabric of his suit. But this time, he doesn't even notice my cat. No, this time his eyes are pinned on me.

"James," I utter his name, hoping to break this dark spell that seems to surround him.

"I can't do this, Cerys." His pained words stab me right in the chest, but before I can respond, he continues. "I'm so bad for you, in so many fucking ways, but I can't walk away. I can't not have you in my bed, in my arms. I need you to understand I'm going to fucking break you until there's nothing left of you. I'm going to take, take, and take, until you're nothing but shattered pieces. It's who I am. What I do. I revel in your brokenness."

His words fall silent, and there, in his dark eyes, are glistening drops of emotion.

Although he doesn't allow them to fall. He holds them close, like he does with me. His one hand on my hip, the other on my face.

His calloused thumb strokes over my mouth, "You're so beautiful with all your color and I'm so fucking dead within my darkness."

"Take my color," I breathe on his lips, watching as he inhales me. My paint-drenched clothes, my dirty hair, and my breath I know is pure coffee. All these things I would normally want to hide from someone, from him especially, he takes it in as if I'm a drug.

"What if I take everything? What if I drag you into my darkness? I'm so fucked up, love. There's so much filth and darkness inside me I don't know what sunshine is. At least, I didn't know until I met you," he tells me earnestly. This is my warning. Run. *Go*, my mind tells me, but I don't. I stand rooted to the spot.

"Then take it. I want you to take what you need from me." I nod, smiling up at him, giving him what he wants. I lean up on my tip toes and plant a chaste kiss on his lips. I expect him to devour me, to ravage me, but he doesn't. This time, he slowly savors the kiss, his tongue dips into my mouth, licking against mine in a tangle of desire.

"I'm scared of breaking you."

"I'm already broken," I confess.

He doesn't touch me anywhere by my

face and the gentle grip he has on my hip. Holding me like a glass ornament that could break at any moment. I feel it in the kiss. I feel every emotion he's tried to tell me. This morning, when he had me bent over the sofa, it wasn't a fuck. No, he was trying to tell me what he's saying now. That even though we've known each other for less than forty-eight hours, this is real.

His warmth sears me when he moves his head away, so he can look at me. Everything he's trying to say is right there, in those intense eyes.

His offers a small smile, pleading with only his stare.

But then he begs.

"Don't leave me. Give me a chance."

CHAPTER ELEVEN

JAMES

I'M AN IDIOT.

That thought sang loud and clear in my head over and over and fucking over again all day long. Lorenzo Ricci, during my meeting, droned on about views of the Grand Canal thoroughfare and sunsets that could make you weep. I'd tried to be present and excited about something I'd wanted for so long, but all I could do was force a smile here and there.

I'm simply a shell now.

And the only person who can fill me with life is her.

Cerys Youngblood.

"Don't leave me. Give me a chance," I repeat, my voice gruff with unfamiliar emotion.

She tenses, her bottom lip quivering, and I realize I fucked up. I had a chance at something good and perfect and real, but I crumpled it in my fist just like I do everything.

"Cerys," I plead as she steps away from me. I reach out to her, but she doesn't touch me back.

"Your mind must be a terrible place," she murmurs, her paint-speckled face scrunching as though it pains her. "So why must you spend so much time there?"

I blink at her and swallow. I have no answer.

When she turns, I follow her through the living room and into a studio. She walks over to the canvas she'd been painting and points at it. It's every bit as beautiful as artwork I've spent hundreds of thousands of dollars on before. Except this painting is real. It's climbing past the fibers, dripping onto the floors, and sliding my way. Taunting and mocking. The painting is me.

My eyes are closed in the picture. Brows furled together as if in excruciating pain. Two fists gripping bars in front of me as though I'm imprisoned. My mouth is parted and red is smeared across my face. Her lips. Red lipstick that belongs to her is the only evidence she exists in my dark, awful world.

"You let it control you," she says, her voice biting angrily at me. "Big, strong, beautiful James Darden lets memories dictate his every action and move. You're a puppet, James. This"— she gestures at the art— "controls you. Pulls your strings and makes you dance these dark little jigs."

Her hand falls, and she regards me with a furious glare. I wilt under the anger she wields like a sword.

"I'm done . . ." She trails off, her lip wobbling. "I'm done watching this show."

Hanging my head in defeat, I let out a shaky breath. "I'm sorry."

"Which is why," she states, her voice softening, "you're going to get your ass in that kitchen and let me make you a grilled cheese sandwich. You're going to tell me about yourself. You're going to listen to me tell you stories. Stupid stories. Silly stories. Sad stories. We're done with this little production you've been the master of." I lift my gaze to meet her searing stare. Strong. Confident. Brave. Her lips quirk in a cute lopsided grin. "I'm running this show now."

I have no words.

I simply stare at the brilliant angel blazing her light my way. All my shadows and darkness are being chased away by her. I'm not sure I want to know the man—the real man—who hides behind it all.

She disappears into the kitchen, and I have no choice but to follow. By clipping the strings she claims control of me, she tied them to her own fingers instead. I follow her because I have no choice. But if I did have a choice, I'd still follow.

I pull out a chair and sit. Awkward and uncomfortable at first in the cozy kitchen. But as I look around, I relax. The table has some wear and tear, the chairs don't match, and yet I find myself calmed by it. Soothed by chaos and imperfection.

"Mom taught me how to make these

when I was ten. I was so proud that I learned how to cook I made them for every meal. Each night, I forced my parents to eat grilled cheese sandwiches until one day my mom had had it. She told me enough was enough." She looks over from the pan where she's cooking and grins. "She taught me how to make grilled ham and cheese then."

My lips tug at one corner when she snorts with laughter.

"Mom died five years ago and . . ." She shrugs, but I can hear the pain in her voice. "I've been lost without her."

A chair scrapes, and it takes me a moment to realize I've risen from my seat. It's like I crave to comfort her on a cellular, subconscious level.

"Sit," she orders.

But I can't. I need to touch her.

Stalking over to her, I rest my chin on her head and watch her as she cooks. The smells are heavenly, but the way she works away without a worry in the world is even better. I want to roll around in this ease that seems to hover around her like a sweet fog. I want it to cloak me too.

"The key to cutting a perfect grilled cheese sandwich," she explains as if I have been wondering all my life about these things, "is a good spatula. This metal one is the right size and kind of sharp." She slides the sandwiches onto two plates, and I watch with amusement as she uses the spatula to cut the sandwiches in two rather than using a knife. Hot cheese melts from the center, and my stomach grumbles.

She laughs, and my chest clenches with joy. "That's what I thought, big boy. Sit down."

Reluctantly, I pull away from her and take my seat. She flits about the kitchen grabbing chips and pouring milk. Eventually, she takes her seat beside me.

She babbles on about her friend named Saskia and a show called Big Brother and how her cats Beavis and Butt-Head came to get their names. I try to listen but only hear bits and pieces. I'm too busy staring at the crumbs on her lips, desperately wanting to lick them off.

"Pop quiz," she announces.

I blink at her in confusion. "What?"

"For someone ultra-focused, you sure do retreat inside of that head of yours. Are you paying attention to me?"

"You're all I see."

Her lips spread into a wide grin. "Okay, fine. I'll let you off the hook because that was really sweet." A blush blooms across her cheeks. "Come. I want to show you something."

She walks. I follow.

Inside her messy room, I should be twitching and angered. I'm a clean freak by nature. Messes and me don't mesh well. Yet, this messy, crazy, horribly dressed girl is in my world wreaking all kinds of havoc, and it's addictive. I don't want it gone. I want more and more and more of it.

"Get comfy," she instructs. "We're going to watch movies and cuddle."

I let out a snort. "I don't cuddle."

Her hands go to her hips, and she juts them out to the side as she arches a brow at me. "You do now, Stalker Darden." Then she waves over at the bed. "I'll be back."

I strip down to my boxers while she showers in the bathroom, and my mind races. I'm in unchartered waters here, and I'm fucking sinking. The thought of climbing out of her lumpy bed and dressing in an effort to retreat back to my comfort zone is strong.

But then she prances back into her room, beautiful and brilliant and bright, and I'm resuscitated. No longer drowning. No longer panicked and confused.

I'm mesmerized.

Her robe is silky and transparent. I can see the shape of her naked body underneath perfectly. She starts a movie and then climbs into bed with me. Her legs tangle with mine as she settles herself at my side.

My cock is rock hard, and my heart is galloping.

I want to pin her down and fuck my crazy into her. Make her see it's not all sunshine and rainbows. It can't be wiped away by a movie called *The*-motherfucking-*Notebook*.

But her sighs . . .

Goddamn, those sighs.

Happy. Content. Relaxed.

I want to breathe them in and live off them.

"Cuddling," she explains. "You're supposed to relax. It's supposed to calm you."

With her palm splayed on my bare chest, I can feel my heart beat slowing. She remains still, and I find myself engrossed in the movie. A fucking movie. It isn't until the credits roll and my little snorer drools on me that I realize—I can do this. I think. I fucking hope. I'll try my damnedest, that's for sure.

Hank, the curious little fucker, jumps on the bed and curls up against her back. Evidently, he knows all about this cuddle shit and is a fan.

Hank may be a texture man . . .

But I'm a cuddle man, it would seem.

I smile at the fucking cat.

CHAPTER TWELVE

CERYS

I ROLL OVER IN BED, REACHING FOR JAMES, BUT find his side of the bed cold. His side. I make it sound like he belongs there. As if he's spent night after night next to me, holding me. But it's not like that. Last night was the first time I ever fell asleep next to another human being in this bed.

Even when Saskia stays over, she has the guest room.

Attempting to ignore the ache in my

chest, I swing my legs over the edge of the bed and pad into my en suite bathroom. Brushing my teeth, I glance in the mirror, noticing the bright red mark on my chest. Teeth marks. He really did mark me. But then he left.

Even though we didn't have sex last night, just falling asleep in his arms was something surreal. Never did I think I would ever be in this position. Falling for a man twice my age. Okay, more than twice my age. But it doesn't matter because even after our admissions last night, he left.

Once I've freshened up, I head toward the kitchen and am halted in my tracks when I find James dressed in only his black slacks and nothing else flipping pancakes.

He doesn't see me as he moves around my kitchen as if he's always been there.

I can't help just watching him. Reveling in his happiness. It hangs around him like a cloud, light, fluffy, and white. Last night he seemed haunted, almost as if he was forever in darkness, and that's when I decided to drag him from it.

If I had to offer up whatever light he saw in me just to see him smile, I'd do it. He spins on his heel finding me staring at him. I'm dressed in just my floppy gray sweater and knee-high black-and-white striped socks.

"Good morning, sunshine," he offers with a lopsided grin that makes him look far younger than his forty-something years.

"I thought you'd left," I tell him, sliding over the laminate flooring and settling on one of the stools which stand at the counter.

"You made me dinner. The least I could do is cook you breakfast." He stacks two plates high with hot pancakes, syrup, and some fresh cream I didn't even know we had. "Your kitchen is a breeze to work."

"You work a kitchen?" I giggle as I take a bite of the pastry on my plate. Flavor bursts on my tongue, and I can't help moaning out loud.

"If you keep making those sounds, I'll be working you, sweet girl." He leans in, planting a kiss on my forehead. The gesture is sweet, almost romantic.

"I thought you weren't the romantic type?" I question in between mouthfuls of delicious pancakes dripping with sugary syrup and heavily whipped cream.

He glances at me then. A cloud of worry and darkness changes his carefree tone and attitude, and I'm afraid I've fucked it up. Silence stills us for a moment, but then, he offers a smile. "I wasn't. Things change. Apparently, an old dog can learn new tricks." He chuckles. He fucking chuckles, and the sound fills my heart with happiness.

"So that makes me the owner, right?" I taunt, teasing him as I watch him inhale the breakfast on the plate. "Jesus, Stalker Darden. Better be careful learning all these new tricks. I might miss the grumpy old fucker who stole me from my apartment and took my virginity." My sassy remark earns me a hungry glare.

"Don't tempt me, love. I'll put you on this counter and eat that sweet little cunt next," he growls, rising from the stool and heading toward the coffee machine.

His promise is illicit and filthy, but my body is already responding in kind. Needy and achy. Who knew one good session of sex could turn me into a wanton slut. I'm turning into Saskia.

I watch him pouring two large mugs of freshly brewed java, deciding now is the time to tell him. "I told my best friend about you,"

I say in conversation.

He stiffens. "And?"

"She reckons you're just scared of feelings. Any normal man is apparently," I inform him, grabbing my mug from his offered hand and sipping the thick, dark liquid.

"I'm not normal, Cerys. I told you, there's so much you don't know about me." This time, he is serious. There's no longer the carefree fun from earlier.

"Then why don't you tell me. I'm not here to fix you, James, but I'd like to know who I'm falling for." The words tumble from my mouth involuntarily, and I immediately want to swallow them back in.

He flits his eyes to me. Shock present on his handsome face. His gaze roams mine, as if he's trying to ascertain if I'm lying or not. But I know for a fact I'm not. I am falling. Perhaps I've already fallen.

Immature.

Stupid.

"You're falling for me?" he questions, keeping his eyes on mine, searching, probing with only those dark orbs. They penetrate me more now than they ever did when we first met. They steal my words, grip my throat, and cause my heart to stutter.

"I think so."

"Cerys," he mutters, leaning closer so his face is in mine. Literally, he's all I can see.

"I meant what I asked you in my apartment."

"Before or after you'd fucked me?" I question with a biting lilt to my voice, hoping I sound stronger than I feel. Truthfully, I'm out of my depth. I'm new to all this. Emotion isn't something I know how to handle. Especially when it's this intense. There's nothing that prepared me for the onslaught of emotions that seem to be barreling through me at a hundred miles an hour.

"I want to keep you. Do you know what that means?" he questions earnestly and warily.

"You want to lock me in a dungeon and have your wicked way with me?" I sass.

Another chuckle vibrates through him,

lightening the mood that seems to be clouding the kitchen. The coffee in my hands doesn't calm me like it always does. I doubt anything can.

"I want to lock you away. I want to fuck my fat cock into your cunt and knock you up. I want to see you swell up with my babies. Not just one, Cerys. I want you to give me a family." He laughs wryly. "Jesus," he expresses, raking his fingers through his hair. "Never did I see myself here. Pleading with a girl to have my children, to offer me something I never thought I could give anyone."

"I'm . . . I'm sorry." I don't know why I'm apologizing, but it feels like the right thing to do.

"No," James grits out. "Never apologize for the way you make me feel."

He reaches for my face, cupping my cheek in his large hand, and pulls me to him. Our lips meet in a heated kiss. I moan, parting my lips for his tongue to enter. To explore and delve into my heat. My warmth.

His low growl is enough evidence that I please him. I offer him something no woman he's ever been with has ever given, and that in turn gives me confidence. I've always been afraid. A little nerdy girl with weird clothes.

The artsy one.

The girl they made fun of.

Many times, I've run home after school

in tears because I was the weirdo all the kids picked on. Called names. But now, now I'm here with the most amazing man, and he cares for me. He wants to claim me and make me his.

When he finally pulls away, his eyes implore me wordlessly to say yes. He's begging. This time, I'm the one in control. But as the moment passes, I realize I was always in control.

James never took, he never forced, and the way he bombarded into my life wasn't done violently. He did it lovingly even if he'll never admit it. He is a romantic. I see it in the way he now asks me for permission.

I nod.

"Are you going to make love to me now?" I question, earning me a sexy chuckle.

"Little girl, I'm going to make love to you. I'm going to eat your sweet little pussy, then I'm going to claim that tight asshole until you're chanting my name like a prayer," he promises, causing me to blush at his filthy words.

"I'm not religious at all," I bite back as his hands find my hips.

"Today, all day, you'll find God again, and his name is James."

With that, he lifts me off the stool and walks me back to my bedroom.

EPILOGUE

JAMES

Six months later . . .

"Y OU'RE A STALKER, DARDEN," I grunt as I tap away on my laptop without looking up.

Her laughter fills my soul. "You're my muse. What can I say?" she teases. "I didn't think you noticed me staring at you anyway. You're quite distracted over there."

I snap my gaze to her and revel in how

beautiful she is on the balcony of our rented flat in Venice. She belongs here. A part of the picturesque world around us. Today, she's wearing a pair of overalls and a yellow tank top. Her red-and-black streaked hair is piled messily on top of her head. Orange paint is smeared across her cheek, but it suits her. "I miss nothing," I remind her. "Show me what you're working on."

She grins at me. Wide and full of perfect teeth. Lips painted matte red, and my cock twitches knowing how many times she's stained it with that exact shade. "You. Always you. You're quite popular over here in this city."

I arch a brow at her and snap my laptop

closed. The contracts on the new hotel have been finalized, and I have bids from builders that need going through, but none of that matters right now. Right now, all that matters is my girl. "I'm only popular with you. Nobody else cares about my broody ass."

"Then how come I sell out every time I put paintings of you in the shop down the street, hmmm? I think other people are fond of your gloom and doom too. Not just me." She turns her painting to where I can see. Mr. Ricci was correct. The sunsets here will make you weep. But seeing how she views me in front of one is breathtaking. I get glimpses of the man that hides inside through her art—only the man she gets to see. And apparently a few locals who buy her art, it would seem.

"You trick them," I grumble. "You make me look like that." Something worth seeing. I wave at the picture where I'm smirking. I'm not wearing a suit but jeans only. My bare feet are kicked up on the railed balcony, and my laptop is in my lap. I look relaxed and happy and free. "Does my hair really look like shit?"

She laughs, and I can't help but smile. "Yes, it does. But I love it."

"What happens when you grow tired of painting me?" I ask as she rises from her seat.

"Never," she assures me. Fierce and protective. Protective over me. My cold heart warms each day I spend with her.

She straddles my lap and runs her fingers through my messy hair. I love her chaos. Her disorder. Her paint splattered all over my dark world. Our flat here in Venice is a fucking nightmare of a mess, and I've never been so at home.

"Did you talk to your dad?" I ask, remembering he called earlier.

"Yeah, he and Liv will be up for Christmas, he said."

"Good," I reply and genuinely mean it. Her father and I may have nearly gotten in a fist fight the first time we officially met a couple weeks after Cerys and I started dating, but we eventually got past our differences. I suppose catching some old-ass man plowing your daughter up against the living room wall one day isn't exactly the best way to meet for the first time. And then waltzing his daughter in front of him not only wearing my ring but my last name, too, a week later also didn't help. But when he realized how happy she was, he eventually caved. I've even shared a couple of drinks with him on occasion. Baby steps.

"When do we have to meet Mr. Ricci and his wife for dinner?" Cerys asks as she starts peppering kisses all over my now-scruffy face.

"In a couple of hours. You better get cleaned up." My palms grab her ass through her overalls, and her breath hitches.

"Maybe I want to get dirty first, Stalker Darden," she purrs, her hips rocking against me as she grinds against my erection in my jeans.

I reach up and unhook one side of her overalls and then the other. Once I've peeled it down past her stomach, I lift her tank top and admire *my* art. "I think you're bigger today," I state, marveling at the silvery stretchmarks on her stomach. "Your tits certainly are."

She laughs and swats my shoulder. "Hey now, asshole. Watch it."

"You're beautiful, love," I mutter, suddenly struck by how very lucky I am. Cerys is mine. My motherfucking wife. And the mother of my child.

Her daddy and I didn't share a drink over that development, that's for sure. In fact, he spent the better part of the day threatening me within an inch of my life for knocking up his daughter.

"So are you," she expresses, her voice growing serious.

"What if . . .?" I trail off. I can't even say the words. But she knows. She always knows.

"Never," she assures me, her voice strong and firm. "You're not like him."

When I finally broke down and told her about the demon who haunted my past, she cried. She cried for the little boy who didn't get to just . . . be. I was driven to be a man from an early age. I never got to just live in the moment. Slowly, Cerys has taught me how to live. Day by day. Minute by minute. We spend our time together, unraveling tiny facts about us. Our past. Our present. Hope for our future.

"You're right," I tell her as I stand with her in my arms. Even big and pregnant, my sweet love is easy for me to tote around. "I will do everything in my power to make this child feel loved. I'll never hurt him," I vow.

She hugs me tight as I carry us to our room. "I know, James. I know this because I base how you'll love him on how you love me. It's unwavering and unbreakable. I don't doubt it for a minute."

I set her to her feet beside the bed and strip down my wife. She's not shy about doing the same for me. When we're both naked, we crawl into our unmade bed. Since being pregnant, she likes being on top. I love being able to watch her fat tits bounce and her lips part when she loses her mind to ecstasy.

Her eyes lock with mine as she rubs against my aching cock. Fingernails dig into my chest as she teases me. Her cunt is drenched, and she rubs her wetness against my dick in a way that maddens me in the good sort of way.

"I love you," I blurt out. Sometimes it comes tumbling from my lips at the most random times, but if I don't tell her, I'll fucking die.

Her lips curve into a smile. "I love you too."

She continues her teasing, sliding against me. "Everyone thought we were crazy," she says, her voice breathless. "Instalove, they said. Nobody falls in love at first sight. That's for movies and books."

I groan when she lifts her body and grips my dick to guide it inside her tight hole. She seats herself on my thickness, and the way her body clenches around me has me nearly blowing my load immediately. Thankfully, she remains still, giving me a moment to compose myself.

"Our kind of love is the kind of love

people create art about," she tells me. "It's messy and confusing. Splashes of color and smears of black. It's deep and meaningful, and if people will just take a moment to truly see it for what it is, they will understand it. Not just understand it, but feel it. A love like ours can't be ignored."

Reaching up, I grip her dainty neck and draw her to me. Her stomach is big between us and I've never been so happy. My lips brush against hers, and I smile.

"We never had a chance to ignore it," I agree.

She kisses me deeply, her hips rocking against me. Then she pulls away. "No, love followed us, beat down our door, and forced its way in." She winks. The irony is not lost on me.

"Meow," Punky Brewster cries from the floor.

Cerys giggles, and I flip off my cat. "Privacy, Punky. We've talked about this."

When I saw the stray black cat a few months ago near our flat with red paint stuck in its fur, I knew I had to get her. Cerys had to leave her four cats with her dad until we get properly settled in Venice, so I knew she was sad. Punky cheered her right up.

Cerys rocks harder against me, her tits bouncing, and I'm stunned by her beauty. We get lost in our own little world, and soon we crash. But at least we crash together. With my cum running out of her, my wife slides off my cock and curls up against me. Our son moves in her belly, pressing against my ribs, and I smile.

He's a cuddle man, it would seem.

Just like his daddy.

ENJOYED THIS BOOK?

MEET THE FOUR FATHERS

Four Fathers Series by bestselling authors
J.D. Hollyfield, Dani René,
K Webster, and Ker Dukey
Four genres.
Four bestselling authors.
Four different stories.
Four weeks in April.
One intense, sexy,

thrilling ride from beginning to end!

These books were designed so you can read them out of order. However, they each interconnect and would be best enjoyed by reading them all!

She's not into him.
He doesn't care.

BLACKSTONE

A FOUR FATHERS STORY

J.D. HOLLYFIELD

BLACKSTONE

BY J.D. HOLLYFIELD

Contemporary Romance

I am meticulous. Structured. A single father.
I obsess over things and crave control.
And when a hot, feisty little woman throws a
wrench in my carefully laid out plans,
I lose my mind.
My every thought revolves around making her
bend to my will—until they become less about
her doing things my way and more about just
her.
My name is Trevor Blackstone.
I am an obsessive, complicated, demanding
man.
People may not understand me, but it doesn't
stop them from wanting me.

KINGSTON

A FOUR FATHERS STORY

She works for him.
He doesn't care.

DANI RENÉ

KINGSTON

BY DANI RENÉ

Erotic Romance

I am arrogant. Insatiable. A single father.
I desire things that would make
most people blush.
Normally, I find outlets that allow me to
free the sexual beast living within and play to
my heart's content.
And when my voluptuous, innocent assistant
starts starving me after a little taste, I decide I'll
let my inner animal feed—on her.
Trouble is, once I have her, I can't let her go,
and that makes things complicated.
My name is Levi Kingston.
I am a dirty, ravenous, greedy man.
People may detest my kinks, but it doesn't stop
them from wanting me.

PEARSON
A FOUR FATHERS STORY
She's too young for him.
He doesn't care.
K WEBSTER

PEARSON

BY K WEBSTER

Taboo Romance

I am selfish. Spoiled. A single father.
I do what I want because I can.
One of my four sons is dating the hot,
young little neighbor...
Too bad it won't last long.
When I want something, I take it—even if it
means taking from my son.
My name is Eric Pearson.
I am an unapologetic, egotistical,
domineering man.
People may not like me,
but it doesn't stop them from wanting me.

She's not his.
He doesn't care.

WHEELER
A FOUR FATHERS STORY

KER DUKEY

WHEELER

BY KER DUKEY

Dark Suspense

I am dark. Calculating. A single father.
I have secrets that would horrify most people.
Stalking is a habit I refuse to break—and what
happens after is a sweet reward.
My life is exactly the way I have designed it.
But an undeserving, sick monster is dating my
only daughter.
Until I deal with my problem, I can't truly enjoy
everything I've created.
My name is Jax Wheeler.
I'm a twisted, evil, insane man.
People may be afraid of me,
but it doesn't stop them from wanting me.

ABOUT
DANI RENÉ

Dani is an international bestselling author.
A proud member of the Romance Writer's
Organization of South Africa (ROSA) and the
Romance Writers of America (RWA).
A fan of dark romance that grabs you by the
throat and doesn't let go. It's from this passion
that her writing has evolved from sweet and
romantic, to dark and delicious. It's in this world
she's found her calling, growing from strength
to strength and hitting her stride.
From the feisty heroines she delivers to the
dark, dominant alphas that grace the pages of
her books, she promises light in a world filled
with danger and darkness.
She has a healthy addiction to reading, TV
series, music, tattoos, chocolate, and ice cream.

*** Get a free exclusive novella by signing up to
my newsletter - http://bit.ly/2sAy5dU ***

BOOKS BY DANI RENÉ

Standalones
Ace of Harts
Love Beyond Words
CUFFED
Fragile Innocence (A dark ménage romance)

Sins of Seven Series
Kneel (Book #1)
Whisper (Book #2)
Indulge (Book #3)
Ruthless (Book #4)

Four Fathers Series
Kingston (Book #2)

Taboo Novella's
His Temptation
Austin's Christmas Shortcake

Crime & Punishment (Newsletter Exclusive)

Carina Press Novella's
Pierced Ink
Madd Ink

Broken Series
Broken by Desire
Shattered by Love

The Backstage Series
Between Love & Fire
Between Lust & Tears
Between Want & Fear

Forbidden Series
From the Ashes - A Prequel
Crave (Book #1)
Covet (Book #2)

Anthologies
When the Dark Wins
Infamous Hearts
Sirens of SaSS

STALK
DANI RENÉ

ABOUT
K WEBSTER

K Webster is the USA Today bestselling author of over fifty romance books in many different genres including contemporary romance, historical romance, paranormal romance, dark romance, romantic suspense, taboo romance, and erotic romance. When not spending time with her hilarious and handsome husband and two adorable children, she's active on social media connecting with her readers.

Her other passions besides writing include reading and graphic design. K can always be found in front of her computer chasing her next idea and taking action. She looks forward to the day when she will see one of her titles on the big screen.

Join K Webster's newsletter
(http://bit.ly/KWebsterNewsletter)
to receive a couple of updates a month
on new releases and exclusive content.

BOOKS BY
K WEBSTER

Breaking the Rules Series:
Broken (Book 1)
Wrong (Book 2)
Scarred (Book 3)
Mistake (Book 4)
Crushed (Book 5 – a novella)

The Vegas Aces Series:
Rock Country (Book 1)
Rock Heart (Book 2)
Rock Bottom (Book 3)

The Becoming Her Series:
Becoming Lady Thomas (Book 1)
Becoming Countess Dumont (Book 2)
Becoming Mrs. Benedict (Book 3)

War & Peace Series:
This is War, Baby (Book 1) - BANNED (only

sold on K Webster's website)
This is Love, Baby (Book 2)
This Isn't Over, Baby (Book 3)
This Isn't You, Baby (Book 4)
This is Me, Baby (Book 5)
This Isn't Fair, Baby (Book 6)
This is the End, Baby (Book 7 – a novella)

2 Lovers Series:
Text 2 Lovers (Book 1)
Hate 2 Lovers (Book 2)
Thieves 2 Lovers (Book 3)

Alpha & Omega Duet:
Alpha & Omega (Book 1)
Omega & Love (Book 2)

Pretty Little Dolls Series:
Pretty Stolen Dolls (Book 1)
Pretty Lost Dolls (Book 2)
Pretty New Doll (Book 3)
Pretty Broken Dolls (Book 4)

The V Games Series:
Vlad (Book 1)

Four Fathers Series:
Pearson (Book 3)

STALK
K WEBSTER

Facebook
https://www.facebook.com/authorkwebster

Blog
http://authorkwebster.wordpress.com/

Twitter
https://twitter.com/KristiWebster

Email
kristi@authorkwebster.com

Goodreads
https://www.goodreads.com/user/
show/10439773-k-webster

Instagram
http://instagram.com/kristiwebster